BASEBALL HOUR

by CAROL NEVIUS

illustrated by

BILL THOMSON

MARSHALL CAVENDISH
CHILDREN

All rights reserved
Marshall Cavendish Corporation, 99 White Plains Road, Tarrytown, NY 10591
www.marshallcavendish.us/kids

LIBRARY OF CONGRESS CATALOGING-IN-PUBLICATION DATA
Nevius, Carol, 1955-
Baseball hour / by Carol Nevius; illustrated by Bill Thomson.—1st ed.
p. cm.
ISBN 978-0-7614-5380-2
1. Baseball—Juvenile literature.
2. Baseball—Training—Juvenile literature.
I. Thomson, Bill, 1963- ill. II. Title.
GV867.5.N48 2008
796.357—dc22
2007014254

The text of this book is set in Lomba.
The illustrations are rendered in mixed media
    on Crescent 115 Hot Press watercolor board.
Book design by Michael Nelson
Editor: Margery Cuyler

Printed in United States of America
First edition
1 3 5 6 4 2

mc Marshall Cavendish
Children

IN BASEBALL HOUR, we practice skills,
warm up, play catch, and learn new drills.

We jog the outfield, easy pace,
then race our teammates to home base.

We sit to stretch, our legs in V's,
bend our heads down to our knees.
We circle arms and twist our backs,
count off twenty jumping jacks.

Ripped
page.

Feeling loose from head to toe,
we grab our gloves and start to throw.

At first we kneel in pairs close by.
We warm up tossing baseballs high.

We back away for throwing longer.
Baseball arms are growing stronger.

In the cage, bat every ball,
until the coach has thrown them all.

Then fielders field and pitchers pitch,

catchers catch and batters switch.

"Should I run from here to third?"
"Watch me, and I'll give the word."

The batter slams a power hit
soaring past the shortstop's mitt.

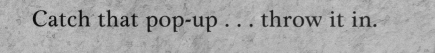

Catch that pop-up . . . throw it in.

Tag that runner . . .

"OUT!"

We win!

Our time is up and practice ends.
Arms like spokes, a wheel of friends.

Teamwork makes our playing power
grow with every
BASEBALL HOUR!